P9-CME-487

ivy + BEAN
BOOK 12

MORE THAN 6 MILLION COPIES SOLD!

* An ALA Notable Children's Book
* A Booklist Editors' Choice
* A Kirkus Reviews Best Children's Book of the Year
* A Book Links Best New Book for the Classroom
* A New York Public Library Title for Reading and Sharing
* A *People* magazine's "Summer's Hottest Reads" selection

ivy + BEAN

GET TO WORK!

BOOK 12

written by annie barrows + illustrated by sophie blackall

chronicle books · san francisco

For the kids who read the very first book about Ivy and Bean a long time ago and the kids who are reading the very last book about Ivy and Bean now and all the kids who joined them in between.
—A. B. + S. B.

Library of Congress Cataloging-in-Publication Data available.

ISBN 978-1-7972-0510-6

Manufactured in China.

Series and book design by Sara Gillingham Studio.
Typeset in Blockhead and Candida.
The illustrations in this book were rendered in Chinese ink.

10 9 8 7 6 5 4 3 2 1

Chronicle Books LLC
680 Second Street
San Francisco, California 94107

Chronicle Books—we see things differently.
Become part of our community at
www.chroniclekids.com.

CONTENTS

THE FIRST PROBLEM

Bean dropped her pencil. Then she dropped her worksheet. After that, there was nothing else to drop. It was time for math.

Carlos earned $3 a week walking his grandmother's dog.

Why doesn't she walk her own dog? Bean wondered.

Carlos wanted a new seat for his bicycle.

What happened to the old seat? Bean wondered.

The seat he wanted cost $14.50.

For a *seat*? Bean thought you should get more than just a seat for $14.50.

How many weeks would it take for Carlos to earn enough money to buy the bike seat?

How should Bean know? Poor Carlos. Was he riding his bike without a seat? Ouch. Maybe if he walked the dog more, he'd get more money. What was the matter with his grandmother? Had she broken her legs? Or was she just old? And what about the dog? Was the dog old, too? Did Carlos have to pick up its poop? Three dollars wasn't very much for *that*. Bean thought Carlos should get a different job. Maybe in an ice-cream store. That's what Bean would do. If you work in an ice-cream store, you make money, plus you get to eat ice cream.

"Okay, people," Ms. Aruba-Tate called. "You should be finishing up."

Finishing? "I'm still on the first problem!" Bean yelped.

Ms. Aruba-Tate clapped her hands. "It's time to come to the rug for a special presentation. Marga-Lee, you are our Colorado today."

Everyone but Marga-Lee groaned. Marga-Lee put her hands in the air and yelled, "I rock!"

The rug in Ms. Aruba-Tate's classroom was a big problem. It had a picture of the United States on it. It was supposed to teach the kids where all the states were. But the kids didn't care where all the states were. The only state

they cared about was Colorado, because it had the Rocky Mountains in it. That meant whoever sat on Colorado got to yell, "I rock!" One day, fourteen kids tried to sit on Colorado at once, and Drew had to go to the nurse's office to lie down. After that, Ms. Aruba-Tate made a "Today's Colorado Is" chart.

Even though none of the other states were nearly as good as Colorado, it was still hard to choose the right one. Bean and Ivy squished into Michigan together. Eric wanted to be North *and* South Dakota.

"People, people!" said Ms. Aruba-Tate. "Sit down! Our special guest is here!"

Everyone twisted around, trying to see the special guest. But it was only the Principal.

The Principal did not sit on the rug. She stood in the middle of the Atlantic Ocean and smiled. "Good morning, second-graders. I see that lots of you are ready to listen. Thank you, Zuzu. And Emma. And Eric. Thank you for being ready to listen like second-graders."

Get on with it! thought Bean.

"Today, second-graders, Emerson School is hosting a special, special event!"

Ivy and Bean exchanged glances. Taiko drumming, mouthed Ivy. Bean nodded.

But they were wrong. "It's a Career Fair!" said the Principal. "Can anyone tell me what a career is?"

"A job," whispered Ivy.

"A job!" called Bean.

"Very good!" the Principal said. "That's right. At today's Career Fair, you will meet people who have many different kinds of jobs, so you can learn all about the wonderful, interesting careers you can choose when you're grown up."

Bean stopped listening. She already knew what she wanted to be when she grew up: an arborist. Arborists climbed trees. They climbed trees and cut off their dead branches with huge chain saws. She could hardly wait.

The Principal was still talking ". . . the PTA has spent many weeks organizing this event, and it is an important learning opportunity, so I expect you, children, to be polite and respectful Emerson emissaries." Finally, she stopped and took a breath. "Does anyone have any questions?"

"Are there rides?" asked Emma.

YOGA, TOOTH DECAY, AND HAIRY PIPES

When Ms. Aruba-Tate's class arrived at the cafeteria, a PTA dad handed each student a pencil and a piece of paper. At the top were the words "When I Grow Up, I Want to Be . . ." The dad explained that they were supposed to list three jobs they had learned about at the Career Fair that they wanted to have when they were grown up.

Bean raised her hand. "Is there an arborist in there?"

The dad frowned. "No, but there's a lawyer."

EMERSON SCHOOL CAREER FAIR!
Your Future Begins Today!

He hurried them inside. The long lunch tables that were usually in the cafeteria were gone. Instead, there were rows of small tables. At each one, there was a grown-up. On every table there was a sign saying the grown-up's name and job.

"Wander around, kids!" urged the dad. "Ask questions! Find out what these people do all day! Discover your passion!"

Okay, okay. Ivy and Bean stopped at the first table. On it sat a tall woman. Her sign said, "Sheila, Yoga Instructor."

She stared at them. They stared at her. "Take a brochure," she said eventually. They took a brochure.

Chet, Banker was next. He had a stack of play money in front of him. "Where does money come from? Answer me that!" he said.

"The ATM?" guessed Bean.

Chet, Banker said, "Sure, but why do we have money?"

Ivy and Bean looked at each other. That was something they had always wondered!

Chet, Banker slid a play dollar toward each of them. "Let's say you have a dollar," he said. "You can keep your dollar safe at home, and you will have a dollar. You can spend your dollar, and then you will have nothing. Or! You can put your dollar in the bank and let the bank use it. To say thanks, the bank will give you a little bit more money. And so, in the end you have *more* than a dollar! You're richer!" He smiled. "Isn't that great?"

Bean and Ivy looked down at their play dollars. "How come we can't buy things with this paper and we can buy things with money paper?" asked Bean.

"Who decided it?" asked Ivy.

"I don't know," admitted Chet, Banker. "I really don't know."

"Let's see if there's an arborist around here somewhere," muttered Bean.

"I'm almost one hundred percent sure there isn't a witch," said Ivy. That's what she was going to be when she grew up.

Augustin, Dentist's table had posters of tooth decay and a basket of floss. "If he wants more business, he should give out candy," said Ivy as they hurried by.

Moriah, Architect had some little buildings on her table. She also had big blue drawings of houses that showed where the walls and windows and doors would go. "So far, she's the only one I'd want to be," Ivy said. She wrote "Architect" on her paper.

"Wait!" said Bean, looking ahead. "There's an author!" Ivy liked books. They went to look at Pegeen, Author. On her table

was a big stack of books, but they were all the same book. It was about avocados.

Narvin, Plumber had pictures of horrible things he'd found in pipes, like hairballs. He even had a sample pipe with hair sticking out the end of it. "Don't brush your hair over the sink, okay?" he said.

Ivy looked guilty. Bean told Narvin she didn't brush her hair at all.

"It still falls off your head," he said. "All the time, it's falling and falling." He looked upset thinking about it, so Bean wrote "Plumber" at the top of her page to make him feel better. But she didn't really want to be a plumber.

As they were walking away from Narvin, Plumber, they saw their friend (most of the time) Leo. He was walking very fast, pulling another kid by the sleeve. "Come on!" he was saying. "Hurry up!"

"What's happening?" called Bean. "Where are you going?"

Leo turned around. His eyes were shining. "I found the best job ever! It's in the back. Come on!"

THE BEST JOB IN THE WORLD

Leo was almost running, and Bean and Ivy had to move fast to keep up with him. They scurried past a whole row of careers to arrive at the farthest end of the cafeteria. There were only two tables in this row, and one of them was empty. The other was surrounded by kids. Behind it sat a big old man in a plaid shirt. "Herman, Treasure Hunter" his sign said.

"Wow," said Bean, looking at Herman, Treasure Hunter's table. On it were lots of coins and jewelry speckled with dirt. "This is a job?"

"Yep," said Herman. "Best job in the world."

"He's my grandpa," said a fifth-grade girl standing next to him. Her name was Elza. She had a very long braid. "He takes me treasure hunting on weekends. Don't you, Grandpa?"

"Yep," said Herman.

"And all that money?" asked Leo, looking at the coins. "You just *found* it?"

"Yep," said Herman.

"Grandpa's rich." Elza flopped her braid.

"How do you know where to look?" asked a third-grader named Sienna Kate, crowding in next to Ivy.

"Well—" began Herman.

"You go to places where people lose things," interrupted Elza. "You go to parks and beaches and parking lots and places like that, because people lose things all the time in those places. They lose keys and watches and jewelry. Even rings! We found *this* last weekend!" She held up a ring with a face on it.

"And I got this one," said Herman. He pointed to a little metal race car. "Antique. Worth a bundle. Found it up at the lake."

"But how?" asked Leo. "Do you just go and dig around?'

Elza laughed. "No! We use this!" She pointed to a metal stick next to her grandpa. "It's a metal detector," she explained, holding it up so they could see it. "You hold it over the ground, like this"—she swung it over the floor—"and when it finds metal, like gold, it beeps. *Then* you dig."

All the kids crowding around Herman's table moaned.

"What?" asked Herman. "What's wrong?"

"How much does a metal detector cost?" asked Leo.

"One hundred sixty-two dollars," said Elza. "But it detects in water!"

Everyone moaned again.

Leo shook his head. "I knew it was too good to be true."

"We're kids! We don't have a hundred sixty-two dollars!" Eric yelled.

"That's almost two years of allowance," Marga-Lee said glumly.

Herman frowned. "Hang on just a minute, there." He leaned down, rummaged underneath his table, and brought up a big book. "Look." The book was called *Finders, Keepers!* On the cover was a picture of a hand holding a stack of gold coins. Herman pointed to the picture. "This fellow in the picture, he didn't use any metal detector. No, sir! He was digging out a basement, and his shovel struck metal. *Clunk!*" Herman's eyes got big. "He pulled up his shovel, and there was a gold coin sitting right on the end! So he keeps digging. And guess what!" He looked at Leo.

"He found more?" said Leo.

"He found a hoard," said Herman.

"That means a whole lot," said Elza. "A ton."

"The old-time treasure hunters didn't have metal detectors," said Herman. "They had shovels and they had intuition. That's all you really need."

"What's intuition?" asked Zuzu.

"A hunch," whispered Ivy.

"A hunch!" cried Bean.

"Right. You feel it sometimes . . ." said Herman, looking into space in a mysterious way.

"Yeah," said Elza. "Real treasure hunters have a special sense."

Wow, thought Bean. A special sense.

Ivy nodded. A special sense.

"People have been finding treasure for hundreds of years," said Herman. "They didn't have metal detectors. They used their heads. They thought: Where do people bury things? Where do people lose things? Then they'd go to that spot and dig up the goods. Metal detectors make it easier. Sure they do. But the most important thing?" He tapped his head. "Intuition."

"And a shovel," added Elza.

No one answered. They were all busy

writing "Treasure Hunter" at the top of their "When I Grow Up, I Want to Be . . ." papers.

INTUITION AND A SHOVEL

Ms. Aruba-Tate seemed surprised that all the kids in her class wanted to be treasure hunters when they grew up. Almost all. Zuzu still wanted to be a music video dancer first and a treasure hunter second. Marga-Lee said she would be a mathematician during the week and a treasure hunter on the weekend.

"You're not going to find much that way," warned Bean. "I'm going to be a treasure hunter during the week *and* on the weekends. I'm going to find a hoard."

"Me, too," Ivy said.

"We can do it together," Bean whispered in her ear. "That way we'll find twice as much as everyone else."

"I'm going to find a hoard, too!" said Eric. "I'm going to be rich!"

"I'm going to be rich, too!" said Emma.

"Did anyone talk to the lawyer?" asked Ms. Aruba-Tate. "Or the author?"

"They were boring!" yelled Dusit. "The treasure hunter had gold and diamonds!"

"Yeah! We're going to be treasure hunters!"

"Treasure hunters!"

"TREASURE HUNTERS!"

+ + + + + +

The treasure hunting started right away, at lunch recess. Almost all the second-graders and even some third-graders went to the field of Emerson School and stood there, looking into space. They were waiting for a sense.

Some fifth-grade kids came out to the field with a soccer ball. "What are you weirdos doing?" yelled one of them. His name was Roddy.

"We're getting a sense," answered Emma. "About where to look for treasure."

Roddy threw the ball in the air.

"You're goons," said Roddy. "There's no treasure! It's a school field, and we want to play soccer on it."

"Too bad!" called Bean. "We were here first!"

In the end, Rose the Yard Duty had to

come and settle it. She said they could get a sense on half the field, while the fifth-graders played soccer on the other half. The second- and third-graders trooped to one side of the field and tried, again, to get a sense. It was hard, with the fifth-graders laughing at them.

Emma started swaying. She said swaying helped her concentrate.

Dusit hummed.

Bean stood, waiting for a sense. Nothing. She closed her eyes and tried to make herself get a sense. Treasure, treasure...what would she buy with her treasure? Candy, of course. But what else? Another pogo stick. A leaf blower. An emu. A dirt bike. A whole bunch of rabbits. A zip line. A swimming pool. Two swimming pools! Her life was going to be so great, once she was rich! Oh! Wait! This wasn't a sense! She had to concentrate! She did. Nothing happened. Bean opened one eye a little to see what Ivy was doing. "Have you got one yet?" she whisper-shouted.

Ivy shook her head.

Suddenly, Leo started running. He had a sense! He ran to the big ugly bush that grew beside the fence. He picked up a stick and started digging, digging, digging. Then the stick broke. He found another and started digging, digging, digging again.

Bean stopped waiting for her own sense and ran across the field to see what Leo's sense had come up with. Everyone else came streaming behind her. The fifth-graders stopped playing soccer to watch.

When she arrived at the bush, he had it in his hands: gleaming gold with the words *U-Jet* printed in silver and black letters on it. Leo held it up so everyone could see.

"What is it?" asked Ivy.

"Gold," said Leo. "A gold U-Jet is what it is."

"Gold," repeated Dusit respectfully.

"How'd you know it was there?" asked Emma, also respectfully.

Leo looked mysterious. "I thought about where someone might drop something, and this bush seemed like the right kind of place."

"That doesn't sound like a sense," Bean said. "That sounds like regular thinking."

Leo shrugged. "Whatever. I found gold."

"You didn't find anything!" yelled Roddy from the soccer side of the field.

He threw the soccer ball at them, and then Emma caught the soccer ball and ran away with it, and then the fifth-graders decided to charge them, and then everyone scattered like bugs, and then the bell rang.

As the second-graders were walking back to class, Eric said, "I have a sense that I'm going to find something really good in my grandma's yard."

"I have a sense that I'm going to find some money," said Marga-Lee. "I have a sense that I'm going to get rich!"

Bean and Ivy looked at each other and frowned. They didn't sense a thing. What was the matter with them?

LOST AND FOUND

After school, Bean and Ivy rushed to Pancake Court to get started on their treasure hunting. But once they got to Bean's house, they decided to keep up their strength with healthy food. Healthy food meant fruit. They ate some raisins. Then they ate some pickles, which were sort of healthy, or at least not unhealthy. Then they had some chocolate milk. Milk was good for you.

They spilled a little chocolate milk powder, but fortunately, they licked it up. Even more fortunately, they licked it up just before Bean's dad walked into the kitchen.

"Hi, kids!" he said happily. He was always excited to see them when they came home. "What's the big plan for today?"

Ivy and Bean exchanged glances. They were glances that said: If we tell him what we're doing, he's going to make suggestions. We hate suggestions. Better change the subject.

"Dad," said Bean. "Have you ever lost money?"

"Lost money?" Dad got a grumpy look on his face. "Yes."

"Really?" The things you find out about your own parents! "How much?"

"Two hundred and fifty-six dollars!"

Whoa, Nellie! That was a lot of money. You could buy almost two metal detectors with that. "Where'd you lose it?" Bean asked. She hoped it was nearby so they could dig there.

"Where'd I lose it? Get this!" Bean's dad huffed. "I spent two hundred and fifty-six dollars on printer ink and then—three days later, tops!—the darn printer breaks. And of course, the new printer doesn't take the old ink! Total waste! Complete bust! And would the ink place take the ink back? No! I wrote to the Better Business Bureau, and do you know what they said?"

Bean and Ivy stared at him. What on earth was he talking about? Ivy put her napkin down. "Thank you for the delicious snack."

"Yeah, Dad. Thanks," said Bean, sliding out of her chair. "We're going to go out in the backyard now. To get some exercise."

\+ + + + + +

The shovels were easy-peasy. There were plenty of good shovels in Bean's shed. Now they were all ready! Time to start digging.

Hmm.

Bean's backyard was big. There were lots of places to dig.

The problem was that Bean had already dug in most of them. Under the trampoline? Bean had buried a pair of tweezers and a jar of rice there just last week. Beside her plastic playhouse? There was a big worm pit there. In the middle of the lawn? Bean and Ivy already knew exactly what was buried there: mysterious bones. They sure weren't going to dig in Bean's mom's flowerbeds. And they both knew that if they dug up the patio stones they'd be in time-out land forever.

"Let's go to your house," said Bean.

Ivy's backyard looked like a place someone would bury treasure. It was the same size as Bean's yard but it wasn't full of playhouses and trampolines and flowers and stones. It wasn't full of anything except tall grass. In one corner there was a tree, a perfectly round pond, and a rock, but the rest of it was tall grass.

"Where should we start?" said Bean. "By the rock?"

"Shh!" Ivy whispered. "Let me get a sense first."

"Oh," said Bean. "Okay." She watched Ivy get a sense. Here's how it looked: Ivy stood very, very still with her eyes closed and her arms stretched out.

It was boring, watching Ivy get a sense, so Bean tried getting a sense herself. She closed her eyes, stood still, and put her arms out. Where are the jewels? she thought. She thought hard. Jewels, jewels, jewels. Like a big glittering red ruby. She wouldn't put it in some dumb ring. She'd put it in her pocket, like it was only a toy, and then she'd pull it out and everyone would gather around to look at her glittering red ruby. "This?" she'd say. "It's okay, but you should see what I have at home." They'd be so jealous.

Wait! This was probably a sense! She was getting a sense about a ruby! "Ivy!" she whispered.

"Shh," whispered Ivy. She was still standing with her eyes closed. "I think I'm getting something."

"I have one already!" Bean said. "I got a sense there was a ruby around here, a big one."

Ivy opened her eyes. "Where?"

"I'm not sure where," Bean answered. "You work on that part."

Ivy began to chant. "Ruby, ruby, tell us where you are. Ruby, ruby, are you near or far?"

Wow, thought Bean, impressed. Ivy's a poet.

Suddenly, Ivy opened her eyes. Suddenly, she pointed her finger to the tall grass in the middle of the yard. "THERE!" she cried.

WORM TREASURE

Ivy and Bean loved to dig. They dug and dug, dirt flying through the air. They sang a digging song, "Gold and rubies and rubies and GOLD! Gold and rubies and rubies and GOLD!" and the hole got bigger and bigger. They found plenty of roots; they found some sticks; they found dirt and stones. But they did not find a ruby.

"Maybe the wind blew my hand in the wrong direction," Ivy said after about half an hour. She dropped her shovel and closed her eyes. "Ruby, ruby, tell us where you are. Ruby, ruby, are you near or far?"

Bean waited.

"Ah!" said Ivy.
"No wonder! We need to move over a little. Right there." She pointed to a spot farther away from the fence.

Again, they dug. Again, they found plenty of roots, some sticks, a few bugs this time, and some dirt and stones. Again, they did not find a ruby.

"I'm pooped!" said Bean. "I need a rest."

They rested in the shade of the tree, near the pond and the rock.

"You know," said Ivy. She turned to look at the rock. "If I were going to bury treasure, I'd bury it next to something that stuck out, so I'd remember where it was." Ivy paused. "For instance, next to a rock."

Bean turned to look at it, too. "Or under it."

In a flash, they were on their feet, rushing to the rock. The rock was big, but it wasn't huge. It was about the size of an extremely large dog or an extremely small bear, and if an extremely large dog or an extremely small bear was pushed very hard by two seven-year-old people at the same time, it would roll over. Which was what the rock did, too.

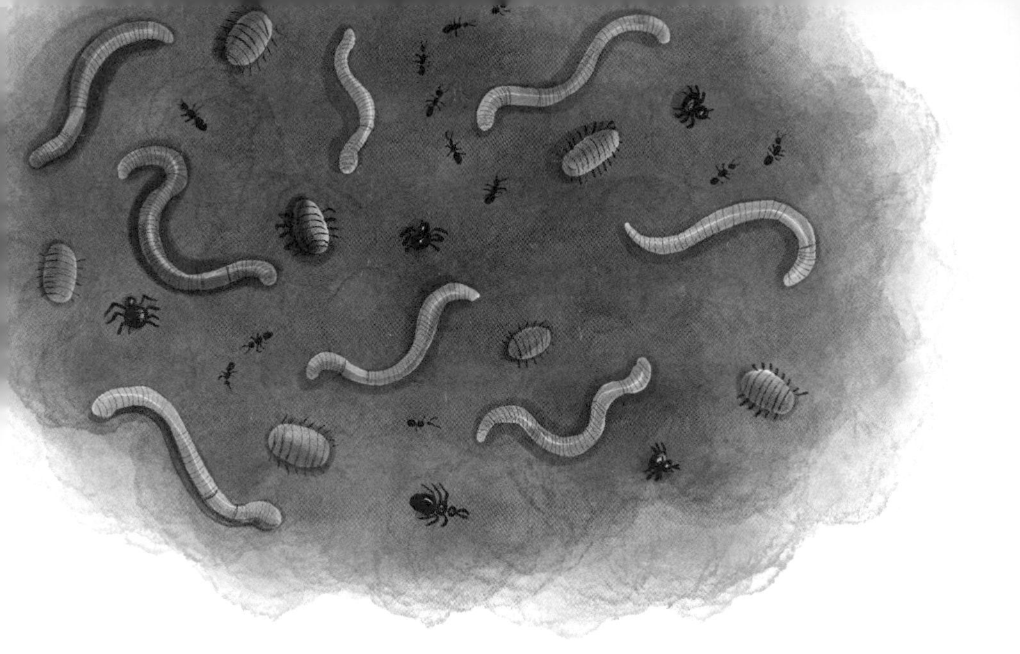

Beneath the rock, a million worms and bugs were crawling and scuttling.

"This is exactly where I'd hide a ruby, if I had one," said Ivy. "I'd bury it and put worms and bugs on top to scare people away." Bean nodded. It was where she would hide a ruby, too. If she had one.

With her shovel, Ivy carefully lifted a layer of wormy and buggy dirt and set it aside.

Bean did the same.

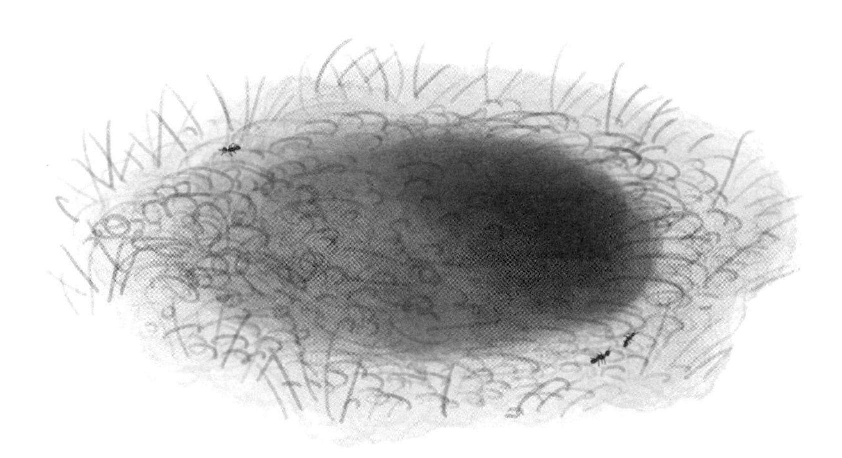

Then they began to dig. This time, they didn't sing their digging song. They just dug. And dug and dug. By the time they had to go inside for dinner, there was an enormous hole where the rock had been. They had found more bugs, more worms, and more roots. But they had found no ruby. They had found no jewels or gold or money. They had found no treasure at all.

+ + + + + +

At dinner that night, when Bean's mom asked what she had done in school that day, Bean almost told her about treasure hunting. Just at the last minute, she decided to keep it a secret. She didn't want to tell her family that her first day of treasure hunting had been a bust. She would wait until she and Ivy found a treasure, something gold and sparkling. She would put it on the table and say, "Look what I found today." Her mom would gasp and ask her how she'd done it. Then Bean would shrug and say, "I just had a sense." And after that, she'd buy everyone presents.

So instead of telling her mom about treasure hunting, Bean said, "I learned you should never brush your hair over the sink." She talked about Narvin and his hairy pipes. Then her dad talked about the time he had taken the sink apart but couldn't get it back together. Then Nancy talked about how much better her life would be if she didn't have to share a bathroom with Bean. Then Bean's mom said that there were plenty of people in the world who would be happy to have any bathroom at all. And then Bean made her eyes really big and said, "I don't mind sharing with *you*, Nancy." And then Nancy huffed away from the table. So everything was fine, and no one guessed that Bean was a treasure hunter, almost a treasure finder.

HOW DIVINE!

The next day before school started, news was passed from kid to kid.

"I found a hoard!" whispered Dusit.

"No way!" gasped Bean.

"Way," Dusit said.

"People!" called Ms. Aruba-Tate. "Are you ready to learn?"

"Yes!" yelled the second-graders.

"A hoard of coins?" hissed Bean.

Dusit shook his head. "Cans. But you can trade them in for money, so it's like finding coins."

"People!" said Ms. Aruba-Tate. "You don't need to be talking right now. You need to be working on your Daily Math."

Okay. Bean tried to concentrate, but all of Carlos's bike-seat problems could have been solved by a little treasure hunting.

Emma leaned over her table. "I didn't find any treasure. I found a little motorcycle I lost when I was five, though."

"Kids!" said Ms. Aruba-Tate. "I don't know why I'm hearing whispers."

Everyone looked down at their papers and tried to think about math. Bean frowned at her paper. Carlos. Bicycle seat. Dog. Okay. Three plus three plus three plus—

Then Eric lost it. "I found gold!" he yelled. "Golden treasure!"

That was when Ms. Aruba-Tate decided to make her classroom a treasure-free zone.

+ + + + + +

So the second-graders had to wait until lunch to talk about treasure. They gathered under the climbing structure.

Marga-Lee held out three quarters, a nickel, and four pennies. "They were right where I thought they'd be, between the curb and the sidewalk. Money always falls out of my dad's pocket when he gets out of the car."

Ivy and Bean looked at each other. Why hadn't they thought of digging between the sidewalk and the curb?

Vanessa had found a plate with a beautiful picture on it. It was going to be worth a lot once she glued it back together. "It's old. My mom says it's an antique."

Ivy and Bean looked at each other. Why hadn't they found an antique?

Eric's gold wasn't just plain gold. It was a gold box with a mirror in it. He'd found it in his grandma's backyard. He said that his grandma's backyard was packed with treasure just lying on the ground. "You don't even have to dig to get rich."

Bean and Ivy looked at each other. Why didn't their grandmas have yards like that?

Leo hadn't had much time to treasure hunt, because of soccer practice. But even so, he had found a silver earring next to the soccer field. "What did you guys find?" he asked, turning to Ivy and Bean.

"Nothing," said Bean.

"Yet," said Ivy.

It was embarrassing to admit it.

It was even more embarrassing when Leo said, "You'll probably find something soon." He was being nice. That meant he felt sorry for them. They had to find some treasure ASAP.

+ + + + + +

By four o'clock that afternoon, Ivy and Bean had dug fourteen holes in Ivy's backyard, three in the front, and one between the sidewalk and the curb. And this is what they had found: half a red plastic comb.

They were discouraged. They were so discouraged they stopped digging and sat on the curb. "We need a metal detector," said Bean gloomily.

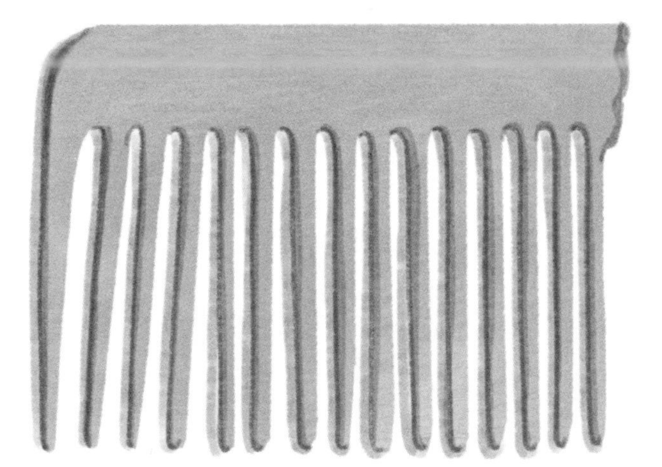

Ivy nodded. "It's not fair. If we find treasure, we'll have a hundred and sixty-two dollars to buy a metal detector. But if we don't have a metal detector, we can't find any treasure in the first place."

"You think a vacuum cleaner would work?" suggested Bean.

Ivy shook her head. "No. That just sucks stuff up. We need something that will tell us where things are buried, like—wait a second!" She slapped herself on the forehead. "A divining rod!"

"A what?" said Bean.

"A divining rod! It's a magic stick that helps you find things!" Ivy said excitedly. "You hold it in front of you and walk around, and it boings up and down when it finds things. Important things, like water and gold. Not dumb things like combs."

Hmm. This sounded a little too good to be true. "Where do you buy one?" Bean asked.

"You can't buy one! They're special sticks shaped like a Y. You're supposed to find them in the forest by the light of the moon."

Bean made a face. "Is your mom going to let you go out in the forest by the light of the moon?"

"Probably not," Ivy admitted.

"Then let's go look in Monkey Park Forest by the light of the sun. Maybe it won't be perfect, but we don't have time for perfect."

The Monkey Park Forest wasn't exactly a real forest. It was more like a bunch of trees planted around the Youth Center. But it looked a little like a forest, and besides, it was fun, walking among the trees, finding sticks. It was way more fun than not finding treasure.

They found a lot of I-shaped sticks. Bean found a C-shaped stick and Ivy found a J-shaped stick.

"What about this one?" asked Bean, holding one up.

"That looks like a Z that got run over," said Ivy. "What about this?"

Bean shook her head. "Keep looking."

"This one is sort of Y-shaped," said Ivy hopefully. But Bean shook her head again.

"Here's a perfect Y." Ivy held up a stick that would have been a perfect Y if one of its arms wasn't missing. "Almost."

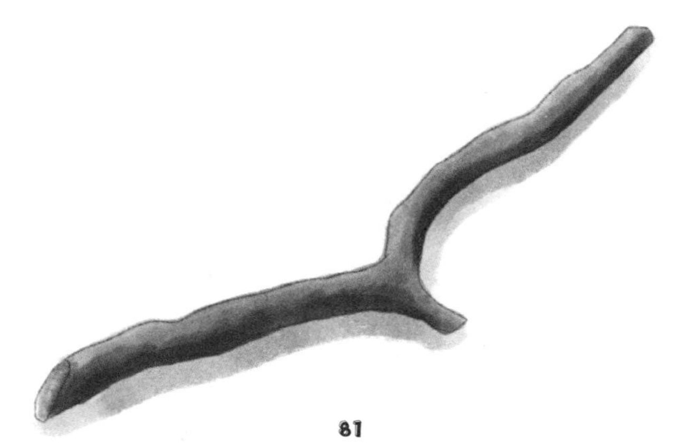

"Look," said Bean. "Let's make it a perfect Y with another stick and some duct tape."

Ivy looked at her almost-Y. "It's the shape that makes it magic. Nobody ever said that *finding* a stick exactly that shape was important."

"Grown-ups say handmade presents are better. Maybe it's the same with magic," said Bean. She grabbed a plain old stick off the ground. It could be the other arm. "Besides, beggars can't be choosers, and we are treasure beggars."

TREASURE BEGGARS

The next morning before school, Ivy showed Bean her divining rod. She had attached the extra arm with plenty of duct tape. Then she had put some fancy gold tape on top of the duct tape to make it look good. After that, she had put star stickers all over the divining rod to make it look even better. And to top it all off, she had used her secret magic book to cast a spell on it.

"What kind of a spell?" asked Bean, touching the beautiful divining rod. It looked like magic, that was for sure.

"A spell to find a lost horse. It was the closest I could get."

"A horse isn't treasure," said Bean.

"If you're someone who needs a horse, it is," said Ivy. "Let's say your car is broken and you have to take your grandma to the hospital. A horse would be the best treasure ever."

"Okay, but I don't need to take my grandma to the hospital," said Bean. "I want gold or jewels or a hoard, like everyone else."

Ivy got a dreamy look on her face. "And let's say you're about to meet the queen, and your hair is all tangled. Then half a plastic comb would be a treasure."

"I don't want a comb!" yelped Bean. "I want treasure!"

"Okay." Ivy stopped looking dreamy. "Don't worry. Now that we have a divining rod, we'll find treasure."

But Bean couldn't help worrying. "We'd better. We have a lot of catching up to do."

By the end of the day, they had even more catching up to do, because everyone else had found treasure galore. Eric had gone back to his grandma's house. This time, he'd found silver. Marga-Lee was six quarters and four dimes richer. She was so rich, she didn't even bother to pick pennies up anymore. Emma had found another one of her old toys. Vanessa was busy gluing her antique plate together. Dusit had twenty-three new cans to add to his hoard. Leo had found a necklace under the sofa. It turned out to be his mom's, but then she gave him fifty cents for finding it, so it was the same as finding money, he said.

Ivy and Bean exchanged glances. They had found nothing. They were terrible treasure hunters.

Worst of all, the other kids decided to have a treasure show at lunch the next day. Everyone was going to bring what they had found and put it out on a table, just like Herman.

Leo turned to Bean. "Did you find anything yesterday?" he asked nicely.

"No," Bean said. She was grumpy. She hated being bad at things. "But you'd better leave a big space on that table for us, because today, we're breaking out our secret weapon."

"It's not a weapon," said Ivy. "It's a divining rod."

"Don't tell him!" said Bean. "He'll want it."

"I don't want it, whatever it is," said Leo, less nicely. "I'm finding lots of treasure all by myself."

"You *think* you're finding lots of treasure," said Bean. She was getting grumpier by the minute. "Compared to what we'll have by tomorrow, your treasure is going to look like a pile of dust."

"Bean?" said Ivy. "It probably won't look like a pile of dust."

"Your treasure doesn't even look like a pile of dust," said Leo. "It looks like zero."

"You'll see!" Bean snapped. "We won't even be able to carry it all. We'll have to get a donkey to carry it for us."

"Um, we probably won't need a donkey," said Ivy nervously.

"You're a donkey," said Leo.

"No, *you're* a donkey!" yelled Bean. She stomped away.

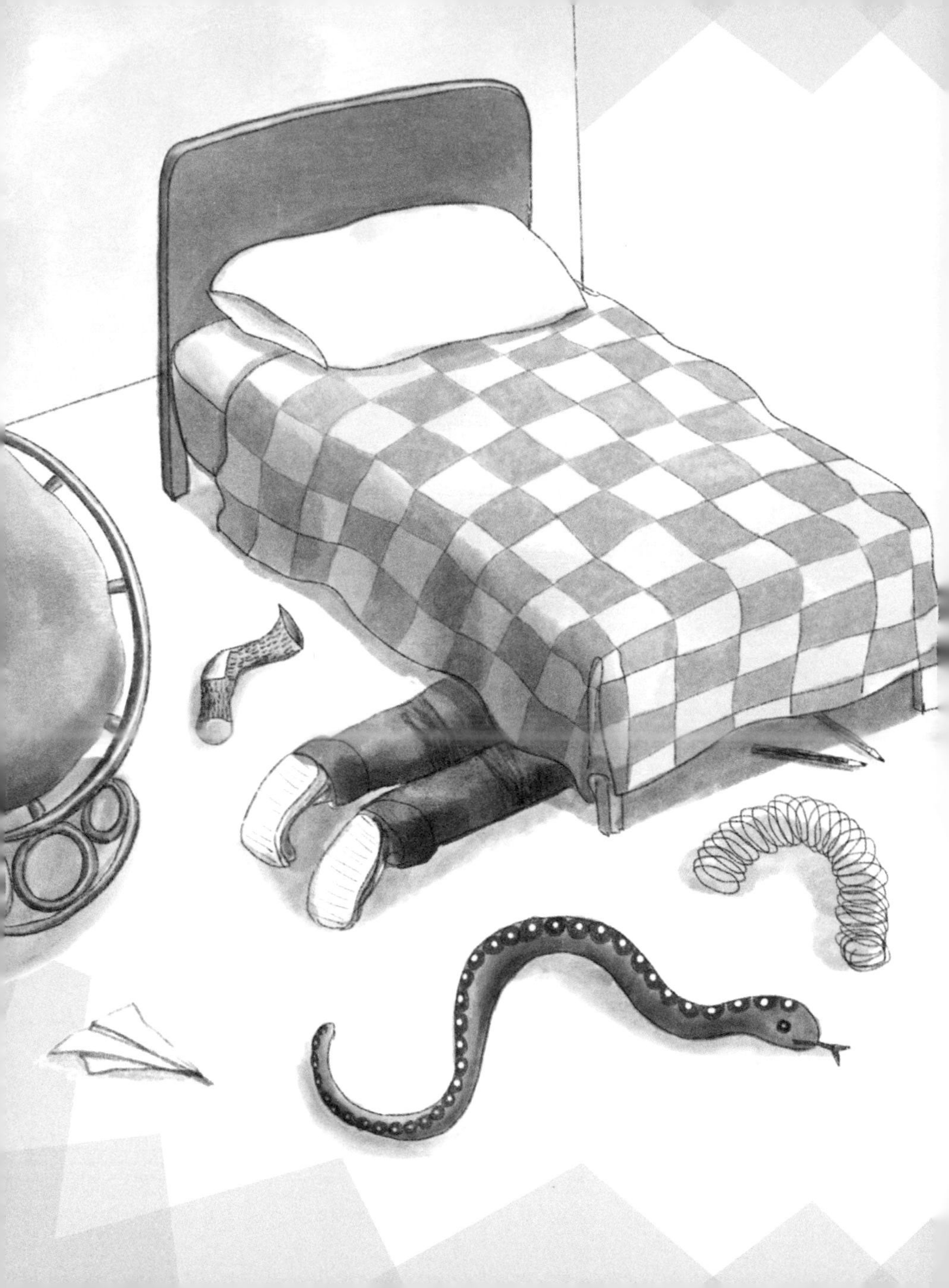

THE SHOE OF PLENTY

Ivy said she had to go to her house before they started divining. That was fine with Bean. She had to go to her house, too.

Once she was there, she scurried upstairs to her room. She knew she had some quarters somewhere, but she didn't know exactly where. Sometimes she hid them in her shoes. Sometimes she hid them in her socks. Sometimes she hid them on the little ledge at the top of her door. It was hard to remember which place she'd hid them last, but boy, no burglar was going to get her quarters.

Eventually, she found them inside a fancy box on her dresser, twelve of them. That made three dollars. She put eight quarters in her pocket. Inside the fancy box, there was a bracelet, too. Bean's great-aunt had given it to her. Bean's great-aunt didn't know Bean very well. The bracelet was made of pink, sparkling shells on pink, sparkling threads. Bean put the bracelet in her pocket, too.

Now, walking very quietly, Bean went downstairs. Without bothering anyone at all, she went out the back door and across the yard to the shed to get a shovel.

+ + + + + +

When Ivy appeared with her divining rod, she said, "I think we should try digging in my backyard again."

Bean said, "I think we should try digging in my front yard."

Ivy said, "I have a sense we'll find something in my backyard."

Bean frowned. "I have a sense we'll find something in my front yard."

They decided to take turns.

In Bean's front yard, Ivy gripped her divining rod with both hands. "You start by standing still," she said. "Then you wait for the divining rod to lead you." She stood for a moment, waiting. "Sometimes it takes a few minutes."

"I'm having a sense that you should be over here, by this bush," said Bean.

"But we don't need our senses anymore," Ivy said. "We've got a divining rod."

"I still have a sense," said Bean firmly. "And you shouldn't ignore a sense."

"Okay, okay." Ivy went to Bean's bush with the divining rod. "Sometimes it helps to close your eyes," she said. "It helps you feel it move." She closed her eyes.

Bean nudged the divining rod with her foot. "It's moving!" she cried.

Ivy's eyes sprang open. "It is!"

"Dig here!" said Bean, pointing to some dirt with leaves on it. She gave Ivy a shovel she happened to have in her hand.

Bean held the divining rod while Ivy dug. And when Ivy found four quarters, she gasped loudly and said, "Money! We found money!"

After that, the divining rod, plus Bean's sense, helped Ivy find four more quarters and, under the camellia bush, a bracelet.

"Nice," said Ivy, putting it on. "Real jewels, right in your own front yard." She didn't look very surprised, though.

"I had a sense they would be here," said Bean.

"It's your turn now," said Ivy. "Let's try my backyard again."

So they did. And there the divining rod, plus Ivy's sense, allowed Bean to find a doll teapot.

"It's an antique!" said Ivy, clasping her hands. "It's probably worth a lot."

"Good," said Bean.

"I'm having a sense that you should take the divining rod over there," said Ivy, pointing to a patch of weeds.

So Bean stood in the weed patch with the divining rod until she felt it wiggle, which happened right after she had closed her eyes. Sure enough, she only had to dig for a moment before she found a big plastic shoe filled with chocolate chips.

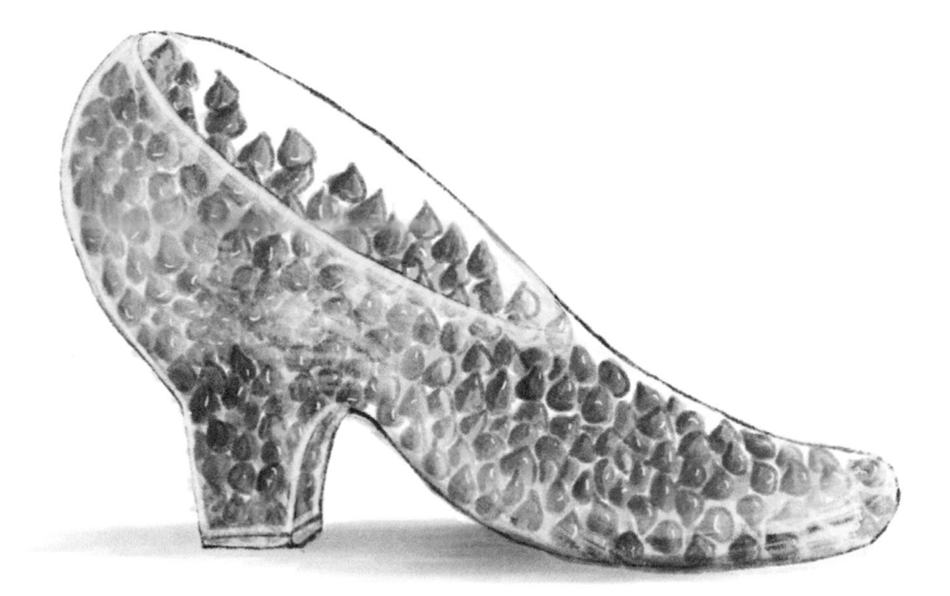

"Wow!" she cried. "Cool!" This was way better than money or antiques! This was chocolate!

"Go ahead and eat it," said Ivy happily. "I'm sure it's still good."

Bean shook the shoe, and a chocolate chip came out the heel. It was still good. "Yum," she said. "This is our best treasure." She shook out another chip. "Have one."

"Thanks," said Ivy.

They sat down side by side in the weeds, eating chocolate chips.

"These are delicious, but maybe we should save some for tomorrow," said Bean between chips. She pictured the big plastic shoe in the center of the treasure table. She pictured everyone admiring it. She pictured Leo looking at it hungrily. She pictured herself giving him half a chip. "Ha!"

Ivy smiled in a satisfied way. "I think we're all caught up, don't you?"

"Sure!" said Bean. "We found money, jewels, antiques, and candy. We're rich."

"There might be one or two more things around here," said Ivy. She glanced at a weed patch across the yard. "But we don't want to be greedy."

"Yeah. It's bad to be greedy," said Bean.

Ivy nodded. "Let's each have another chocolate chip, to celebrate our treasure."

So they did.

SHOWTIME!

Vanessa told the five first-graders sitting under the picnic table that they had to move. "We're having a treasure show," she said.

"But this is our clubhouse," said a skinny first-grader.

"If you move, your club can look at our treasure before anyone else," said Bean.

The first-graders moved.

Each of the treasure hunters got a section of the table. It was a big table, but even so, Dusit couldn't fit all of his cans in his section. He was loaded with cans. He was a can millionaire. He put twenty cans on the table, and the rest stayed in a bag beside it.

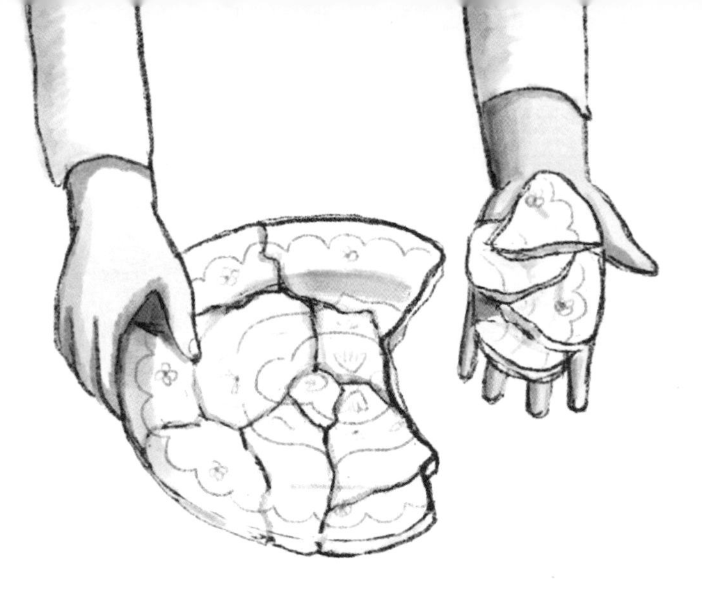

Vanessa was almost done gluing her plate together. She brought the glued part and four leftover pieces. It had beautiful flowers on it and even a golden rim. "Who knows how much money it will be worth once I finish gluing," she said.

Eric brought only his golden box with the mirror. He could always get more treasure from his grandma's yard, he said, whenever he felt like it. He set the golden box in the middle of his section, where it glowed.

Leo brought the golden U-Jet, the silver earring, the fifty cents his mom had given him for her necklace, and a tiny robot he'd found the day before. "I don't think the robot is an antique, though," he said modestly.

Marga-Lee lined up all her coins: quarters, dimes, nickels, and the four pennies she had picked up before she stopped picking up pennies. "It comes to three dollars and twenty-four cents," she said. "Free money."

Emma had forgotten to bring her toy motorcycle and a glass monster she had found, so she drew a picture of them and laid it in her section.

Ivy and Bean shared a section.

Carefully, Ivy lined up her eight quarters in the back. Directly below, she spread out the sparkling shell bracelet. Bean plopped down the antique doll teapot. And then, at the front of the table, she placed the shoe full of chocolate chips.

"Can I have one?" asked Emma.

"Not until the show's over," said Bean.

Since Ivy was a good speller, she had written the sign. It said "Treasure Show," and Bean had drawn flowers around the words. It was very pretty. They taped it to the table.

Then each of the treasure hunters stood behind their section and waited.

The first-graders zoomed over. They looked at the treasure. "How much does the robot cost?" asked the skinny first-grader.

"It's treasure!" said Leo. "It's not for sale."

The first-grader turned to Bean and Ivy's section. "Can I have a chocolate chip?"

"Sorry," said Bean. "It's treasure."

"Food isn't treasure," he said, walking away.

Rose the Yard Duty came over. "Just make sure you pick up all this junk at the end of lunch, kids, okay?"

"It's treasure, not junk!" said Dusit. He pointed to his cans. "These are worth big bucks!"

"Treasure show?" someone hooted. "You call that treasure?" It was Roddy the fifth-grader and his soccer friends. "That's stuff you find in the garbage can!"

Bean was getting tired of hearing this kind of thing. "What do you know about treasure?" she snapped. "Nothing!"

"I do," said a voice. "I'm a treasure expert."

It was Elza, the fifth-grade treasure hunter! She slid in front of Roddy and his friends and flopped her long braid over her shoulder. "Hmm," she said, looking down at the table. She looked down at the table for a long time. "Hmm."

"Well?" said Vanessa. She pointed to her plate. "It's an antique."

Elza made a little sniffy sound. "It's broken. Nobody wants broken stuff. And that," she pointed at Eric's golden box, "is only plastic. Plastic isn't worth anything. If it's not worth money, it's not treasure."

"Cans are worth money," said Dusit.

"Money's worth money," said Marga-Lee.

Elza made a face. "Cans aren't treasure. A quarter you find on the ground isn't treasure. Treasure is something people *want*. Treasure has to be something *good*. Something *special*." She picked up Emma's drawing, looked at it, and put it down. "What's that supposed to be?"

"Nothing," said Emma. She folded her picture in half.

Bean noticed Leo sliding his U-Jet into his pocket.

Marga-Lee put her hands on top of her coins.

Now Elza came to Bean and Ivy's section. Her eyes flicked over the teapot and the coins and came to rest on the bracelet. "Okay, this could be treasure. It's pretty good. Where'd you find it?"

"I dug it up," said Ivy. "In a secret place."

"Cool." Elza picked up the bracelet. "It could be worth something," she said. "You should take it to a jewelry store and ask them what it's worth."

"I don't care what it's worth," said Ivy. "It's my treasure."

Elza shook her head and put down the bracelet. "You guys are completely missing the point of treasure. Can I have a chocolate chip?"

"No," said Bean. "That's my treasure."

Elza smiled. "I wouldn't call chocolate chips treasure."

"I would," said Bean. "I'd double call them treasure."

"I would, too," said Ivy.

They stood next to each other and glared at Elza until she flopped her braid again and went away.

Treasure Show

RICH, RICH, RICH

The treasure hunters sat quietly at the table. Marga-Lee moved her coins around in circles.

"I'm not going to be a treasure hunter anymore," said Dusit. He flicked one of his cans, and it clanged to the ground.

"All that gluing for nothing," said Vanessa.

Bean leaned on her elbows. "I'm going to go back to being an arborist when I grow up."

"This was dumb," Leo said. He pulled his U-Jet out of his pocket. "It's just plastic. I knew it was plastic, but I thought since it was gold, too, it was treasure."

"I thought I was going to be rich," said Eric sadly.

"Me, too," said Emma.

"Me three," said Vanessa. "Ivy's the only one who might be rich, since she's the only one who found real treasure."

Ivy picked up the sparkling shell bracelet and looked at it for a moment. "Eric," she said suddenly. "I'd much rather have a golden box than this bracelet. You want to trade?"

"For sure!" said Eric. He handed her the golden box.

Ivy passed him the bracelet. Then she opened the box and peered into the tiny mirror. "This is exactly what I needed," she said. "I'm going to use it to spy on people behind me."

Bean watched as Ivy set the box carefully in the center of their section. Right, she thought. It's treasure if it's what you want. Bean scooped up four quarters and turned to Leo. "Will you sell me that robot for a dollar?"

Leo sold it for a dollar and three chocolate chips.

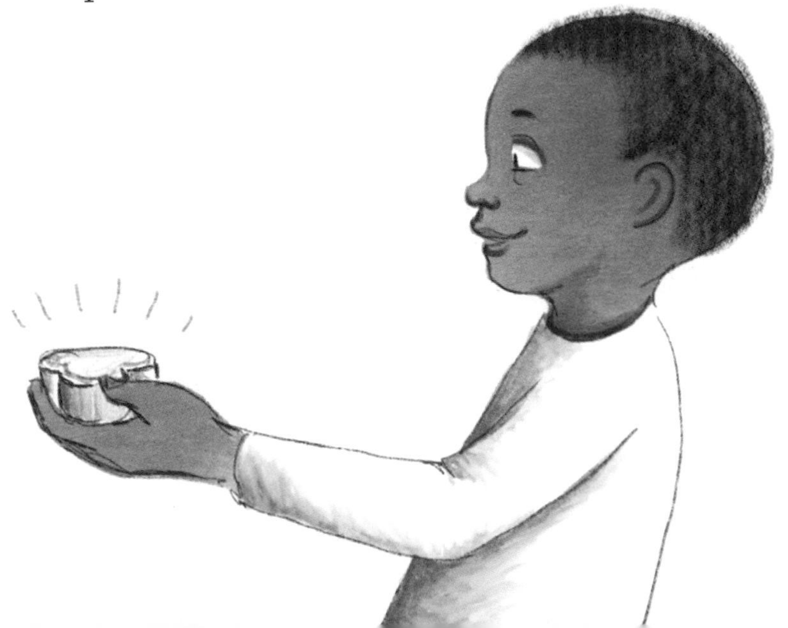

"I'll give you this dollar for your cans, Dusit," he said, munching chocolate.

"Get out of here!" said Dusit. "These cans are worth three dollars, at least!"

"I've got three dollars," said Marga-Lee. "But I want your shoe, Bean."

"*With* the chocolate chips in it?" said Bean. "No way! You can have the shoe empty for three dollars."

"Rip-off!" Eric yelped. "Hey, Marga-Lee, let's go in together. So one bracelet and three dollars for the shoe *and* the chocolate chips."

"Only half the chocolate chips," whispered Ivy.

"Half the chocolate chips!" yelled Bean.

"No!" yelled Eric. "All!"

"How about twenty cans and three dollars and the bracelet!" yelled Dusit. "For all the chocolate chips. And the shoe!"

"Three dollars and fifty cents!"

"I don't have three dollars and fifty cents! Leo! Lend me fifty cents!"

"No way!"

"Get out!"

Pretty soon, everyone was yelling. They yelled for a long time, and when they were finally done, Ivy and Bean had sold all the chocolate chips, the shoe, and two quarters to Dusit, Vanessa, Leo, Eric, and Marga-Lee for twenty-five cans, three dollars, a U-Jet, most of a plate, the bracelet that Ivy had traded in the first place, and ten chocolate chips.

Ivy and Bean divided their ten chocolate chips into two piles of five and popped them into their mouths. Just as they swallowed, the end-of-lunch bell rang. The treasure hunters rose, gathering their cans and coins and antiques and toys into their arms, and began to walk toward Ms. Aruba-Tate's classroom.

With her arms around her bulging bag of cans, Bean walked beside Ivy. She felt happy. She had everything she wanted. "We're rich!" she sang, clasping her treasures. "We're rich, rich, rich!"